This book belongs to:

• • • • • • • • • • • • • • • • •

Rebecca Ashdown

Bob AND Flo
hide and seek

OXFORD
UNIVERSITY PRESS

It was a rainy day.

Bob came to nursery
with his umbrella.

'Hello,'
said Bob.

'Oh, hello!' said Flo and Sam.

'We didn't see you hiding under there!'

Bob and Flo and Sam decided
to play a game of hide and seek.

'I'll hide first,'
said Bob.

Counting to twenty is hard.
So Flo and Sam counted to ten.

Twice!

Bob found an
excellent place
to hide . . .

but Flo and Sam found him
straight away.

'You have
to hide
behind
something,'
said Sam.

So Bob had another go.

But he was still too easy to find.

'You have to **disappear**,' said Flo.

'Oh,' said Bob.
'One more go!'

'Perhaps Bob needs more time to hide?' said Flo.

So Sam and Flo decided to play in the kitchen corner while they waited.

Bob thought very hard . . .

about how to **disappear.**

'Coming,
ready or not!'
said Sam and Flo.

But where was Bob?

Nowhere

to be found.

'TA DA!
Here I am!'

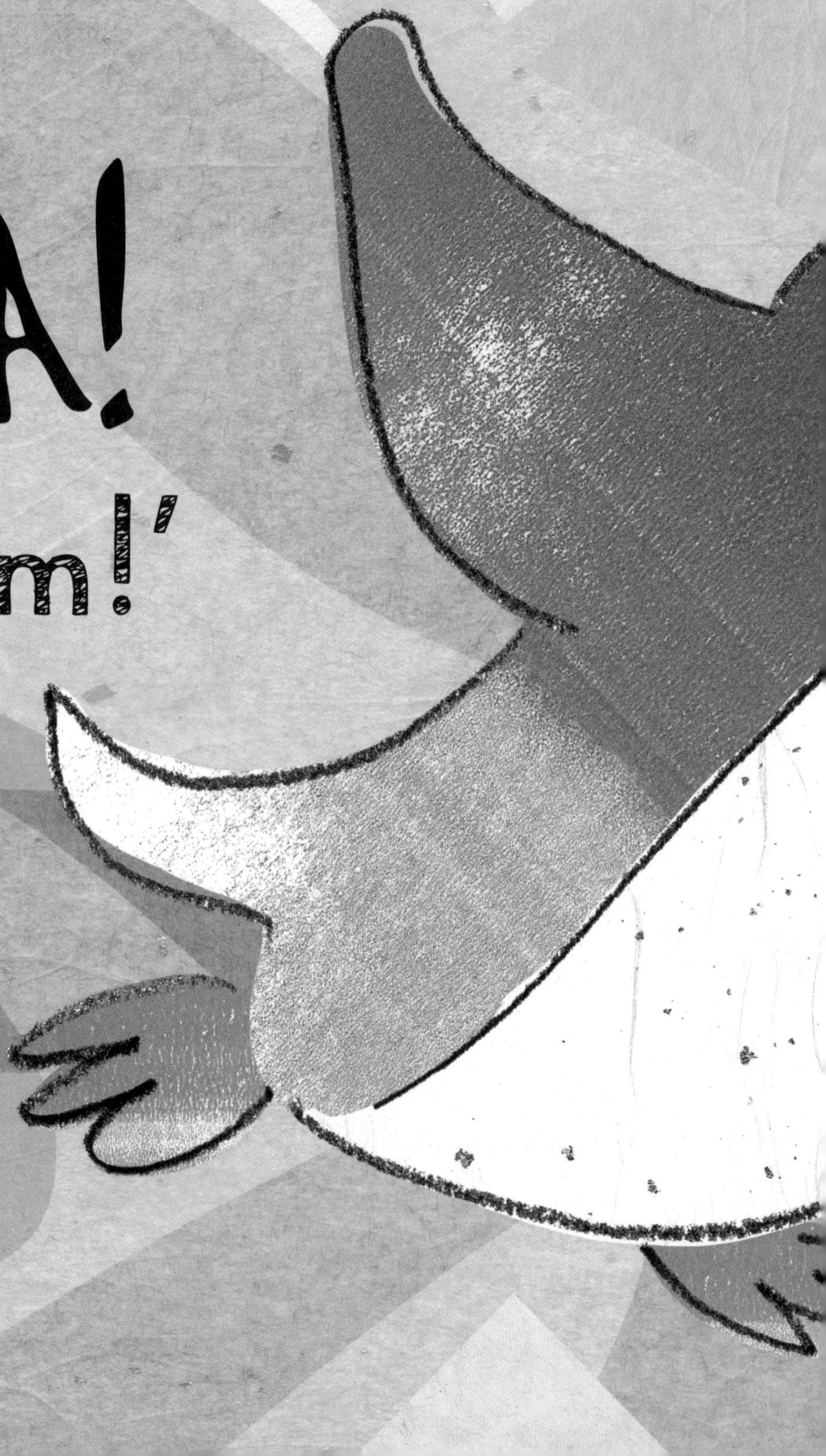

Flo and Sam thought Bob
was **brilliant** at disappearing.

And Bob thought
Sam and Flo's baking

was **just** as **good.**

For Alice, Samson, and Anabel

OXFORD
UNIVERSITY PRESS

Great Clarendon Street, Oxford OX2 6DP

Oxford University Press is a department of the University of Oxford.
It furthers the University's objective of excellence in research, scholarship,
and education by publishing worldwide in

Oxford   New York

Auckland   Cape Town   Dar es Salaam   Hong Kong   Karachi
Kuala Lumpur   Madrid   Melbourne   Mexico City   Nairobi
New Delhi   Shanghai   Taipei   Toronto

With offices in

Argentina   Austria   Brazil   Chile   Czech Republic   France   Greece
Guatemala   Hungary   Italy   Japan   Poland   Portugal   Singapore
South Korea   Switzerland   Thailand   Turkey   Ukraine   Vietnam

Oxford is a registered trade mark of Oxford University Press
in the UK and in certain other countries

Database right Oxford University Press (maker)

This book first published 2016

2 4 6 8 10 9 7 5 3 1

British Library Cataloguing in Publication Data

Data available

ISBN: 978-0-19-273715-1 (hardback)
ISBN: 978-0-19-273716-8 (paperback)

Printed in China

Paper used in the production of this book is a natural,
recyclable product made from wood grown in sustainable forests.